Seconds

"There is a wealth of brave wisdom in this novella. Putnam takes a social encounter and peels back its layers—through time, ancient longings, lingering dishonesties—until reaching unsettling but crucial insights. I love when a short book takes on the truly big issues of human experience, and Putnam's does so triumphantly here."

ROBIN BLACK
author of *Life Drawing* and *If I Loved You, I Would Tell You This*

"*Seconds* is sharp-eyed and wise. It is the perfect vessel for its story of art and tragedy and mis-centered love, of risk and payment due, of the flicker of darkness in us all."

ROY KESEY
author of *Pacazo* and *Any Deadly Thing*

"In *Seconds,* Claudia Putnam gives us a deep, intimate look into the human heart, showing that quick decisions can have lifelong consequences. A beautiful, haunting tale of unrequited love and regret."

SCOTT LASSER
author of *Say Nice Things About Detroit* and *The Year That Follows,*

"In *Seconds,* Claudia Putnam explores passion and the extremes that people—all people—will go to fulfill their desires, hurting the people they love and loving the people they hurt. She is pinpoint in her depictions of these humans she's created, sketching joy and tragedy like an old master.

MICHAEL CZYZNIEJEWSKI
author of *The Amnesiac in the Maze*
and *I Will Love You For the Rest of My Life: Breakup Stories*

"Through the eyes of Putnam's outsider narrator, Ethan Codding, the transgressive darkness just below the surface of New England propriety and privilege seethes, crackles. The story's ageing ensemble takes shape viscerally and quickly in this writer's hands, her cast reminding me of Kingsley Amis's delicately grotesque, flawed crews of wayward, older characters negotiating regret, loneliness, missed chances. Putnam's understated but tangled powerplays between art and money, development and conservation, empathy and obsession, power and trauma contend in an unquestionable New Hampshire landscape—a setting that is essential to our understanding of the human drama she manages so deftly in the novella's compressed space. The fraught aspirations and inheritances of Ivy League boomers, local law enforcement, equestrians, loggers, and academics make for a compelling stew. But, like John Casey's Rhode Island in Spartina, *Seconds* avoids caricature, evokes and respects the subtle diversity and quirks of a regional demographic, its veneer and underbelly. Codding's Western, inverted Carraway-esque perspective injects *Seconds* with remarkably brutal poignancy; the author's conjuring of his brooding about the artist Anna Halloran—the mental and emotional gymnastics of male self-awareness—is nothing short of brilliant."

RALPH SNEEDEN
author of *Evidence of the Journey* and *Surface Fugue*

Seconds

A NOVELLA

CLAUDIA PUTNAM

NEUTRAL ZONES PRESS
2023

Seconds
By Claudia Putnam

Published by Neutral Zones Press
Brooklyn
neutralzonespress.com

Cover and text design by adam b. bohannon
Cover art: *Morning Light*. 28"x 22", oil on linen, by Grace G. Cooper

For any information,
please address Neutral Zones Press: editor.neutralzonespress.com

ISBN 979-8-218-15887-3 (online)
ISBN 979-8-218-15888-0 (print)

For Julian,

who may at times wonder why

he was not brought up

"back there."

Seconds

1.

WE WEATHERED SOME HEAVY RAIN, small hailstones, on our way to visit my old friend John Perkins and his second wife. The roads in that part of New Hampshire are frost-heaved, potholed, the state being tight-fisted, resentful of the public funding of anything, or possibly assuming of drivers' good sense in navigating obstacles on their own. My car hydroplaned through the puddles in the deep shadow of Ranger Mountain. Maybe it was me, maybe I wasn't the driver I used to be. I was thinking about cars, the ways in which one should drive them. I had a luxury performance car, all-wheel drive, neither terrible in weather nor the greatest on the dry roads, but better than your average Camry. I wasn't worried about a thunderstorm, even with some pea-sized hail. Then again, it was no Porsche.

What sort of driver are you? If you owned a classic sports car, would you drive it only on Sundays, fair-weather Sundays, garaging it the rest of the time? If I did have cool old Porsche up here in New Hampshire, I'd like to think I would take it out on the South Road where the curves aren't always banked properly and see how she does. I'd take her over Ledge Hill, Grace Hill, where the turns are hairpin, then past Hanover, down along the Connecticut. You'd want to put a car like that to the test, you'd want to let her shine. Wouldn't you?

I wanted to bring this up, as we drove, with my wife. I almost did. Tina and I used to talk about things like cars, material things, dreaming of owning this one or that. Then we stopped caring, or she did. I stopped caring as much as I once had. Eyesight, reflexes, too many speeding tickets. At some point you realize 85 is about as fast as you're ever going to drive again. As we approached Perkins Lane, the wind tore at the remaining leaves—foliage had not been great this year, having turned early. Tina sat up, not tense, but gathering herself.

Once I thought I was the sort of man who'd own a sports car, who'd open her up, even on a day where there might be a bit of rain. My college roommate, John Perkins, was never this sort of man. I didn't discover this about him till nearly a decade out of school, a hard lesson at a bad time.

I'm not really talking about cars.

When we were young, he did, it turned out, have a Porsche 911 Targa garaged in the barn behind his house. I lived in the apartment above that barn while I was briefly—seemed like forever, then—in business school at Dartmouth. There were also a couple of horses stabled on the far side of the lower level. Just to give you a feel for the estate-like nature of the place. I drove an older Saab 96, one of those models that looked like a fancy bar of soap. I parked it in a wide spot in the circular drive. It was 1979.

John's first wife, the painter Anna Halloran, had a studio in a converted sheep barn not far from the stable/apartment/Porsche garage. On Sundays, she would get in the Targa with him and they would drive around together, I guess along some of the routes I've just mentioned. Maybe up to Conway in the fall to look at the foliage. On Sundays, I would watch them drive off and I would think, Are you kidding?

2.

IN COLLEGE I thought John Perkins was gentle, polite, self-effacing, if holding on to his place at Harvard by the coil of his DNA. Quick to laugh at all our jokes, never quick enough to crack them himself. Always the one to call if you were too drunk to drive yourself somewhere. If you needed a ride from the airport. If you'd done something stupid like got yourself stuck in a blizzard with a motorcycle somewhere, as our Classics-major friend Stickney had done at some hotel in the Poconos with a girl he didn't want to tell his parents about. John especially loved to bail out otherwise brilliant friends who had gone and done stupid things. This meant, we all believed, that he was a nice guy.

Impossible to shake this notion today. You drive up to the house, park in the circular drive. Light gushes down the steps. He comes down them no matter how bad his knees have become. He walks to the door of your car, helps you with the dishes or flowers you've brought, shakes hands all around, even gives you a hug, brushing your ears with his beard, dyed a constant sandy blond. A hug! In New England! That's a function of the second wife, some series of spiritual workshops.

The deep voice hasn't changed. "Ethan Codding!" he says. "It's been far too long. And the lovely Tina!" I read an article on voices, how they depend entirely on the number, positions, and depths of the sinuses. He used to complain about his sinuses. Apparently the new wife also made him get rid of a number of foods, like cheese and wheat. In any event, he still has that rolling tenor that makes you want to vote for him. He wants to know everything, asks after your family, all the old gang. Stickney, he says, with a shake of the head, has never cut his hair. He even tells you all about his first wife Anna, as if they're great friends and talk frequently. Tina looks over at the new wife. Penny follows the conversation bright-eyed. No hard feelings anywhere. And why should there be, with this great old house still perched atop its hill, the Perkins assets still so well managed, so much abundance and fortune everywhere. The children all in college or professional schools now. You don't want to ask after the kids; you'll be up all night.

A person cannot suffer a consequence if he does not even see his mistake. If he does not drive his Porsche on a rainy day in the mountains, perhaps he won't miss it if he wrecks it on the Sunday. He might simply replace it with a Lexus and think he has done just as well. In fact, after John and Anna divorced, he sold the Targa. "It was nothing but problems waiting to happen," he said. "No one around here can work on them, you have to have it flatbedded out. I was always in dread."

So there is no longer any car for luxury outings. Just a reliable Honda SUV, a Volvo station wagon for his new wife. The horses are gone as well. "Too dangerous," the wife has said. Her curly hair has turned an undyed gray.

Inside the house, not much has changed. The ceilings are low by today's standards. Men were smaller in the days when this ancestral place was built. John at six feet is cleared by only another half-foot. This provides scale to the man, which you didn't get out on the front steps. He's paler than usual, seems gaunt. It's been a year since I've seen him; his face is cut with lines, suddenly. Webs reaching into his cheeks, not just the usual places around the eyes and lips. "Something troubling you?" I ask.

He sighs, sidling away from the women. "An incident on the lake is all. Someone scuttled the MayRoy."

What? "Sunk it?"

"Stole it, drove it out a ways, stove it, sunk it."

I'm silent at this, imagining the various angles of that affront. The MayRoy: a century-old Chris-Craft custom-made for the Perkins family. Her low, sleek lines made her stand out among the dozens of other Chris-Crafts that joined the annual parade on the Big Lake. Someone would have had to have broken into the Perkinses' boathouse in Enshaw Harbor. Beyond that transgression, driving a stave through those ancient, lovingly varnished and re-varnished boards would take a certain determination, a willingness to violate beauty and history that you didn't often find in people around here.

"Any idea who?"

"Hard to imagine, but there's an idea or two. No evidence so far." He looks hurt, as if he's been dumped by a lover. "Pure nastiness," he says. "Cops think it's just drugs, kids on drugs."

I don't bother to voice the objection I know he shares. Drugs today, people like to say, are not like *our* drugs. I remembered stumbling around the Harbor on Quaaludes with John. Taking downers—a stupid way to get high if there ever was one. It didn't exactly inspire you to anger. It's true we mostly used downers, hallucinogens. Mellow highs. Coke was common, though, and so was speed. Despite today's prevalence of drugs I've never heard of, or drugs renamed in ways I've never heard of, I think kids are kids. Not many would behave much differently from how we did when we got fucked up in our youths. Nastiness directed at John is probably nastiness directed at John. No matter how unprecedented.

John excuses himself and slips away down the hall, I assume to the bathroom. I almost wonder if he's going to cry.

Penny watches him go. "Things have been very tense around here," she says. "Very tense."

"I can't imagine losing the MayRoy." Harder to explain to people, but much more valuable and far more symbolic than a Porsche.

"Happened last week. Still too raw to discuss."

That leaves me with nothing to say. I walk over to some of Anna's artwork. Her paintings dominate the living and dining rooms. Two significant later works as well as a couple of pieces from their marriage. Had it pained Anna to leave those behind? Had he claimed them in the divorce agreement? Kindly, cheerfully, of course. Because he had come to love them too, he might have said.

What does this new wife think, I wonder, as I often had, trying not to examine the paintings too obviously, in case John comes back and puts his arm across my shoulders, starts telling me how much he loves this or that and why. Or worse, how terrific this piece is because of its use of color or scale or something that can't help but betray his ignorance of what Anna was doing all that time and all this time.

"What happened anyway?" Penny says. She is thin, gray-skinned in that over-drawn way of the aging ultra-runner. Wire and bone. Her voice is at shoulder-level. I tilt my ear to her.

"What do you mean?" The horse in the painting? Its rider?

"I mean why Anna left."

Feeling Tina regarding me as well, I attempt a dismissive shrug. "Divorce. Who knows. Always a host of reasons. You and John must have discussed it."

"Sure, the general reasons for marital failure, divorce. But something happened, I can feel it."

We are standing beneath a painting that had been part of an exhibition I'd long ago seen reviewed in *The New Yorker*. I'd been out of the country while it was shown. This piece, hanging above the plush sofa, had an almost Clyfford Still quality of abstraction to it. In a Still piece, colors will be dark and blotchy. If there are people, their body parts might be disproportionate, cartoon-like. Workers in fields will have long, ungainly, muscular arms. In Anna's work from that time, there was nothing cartoon-like or blotchy, but colors were distorted in their vividness as if you were on acid, or at least stoned. As if the images were straining mightily to compete with the vividness of the life surrounding them.

The painting is 6x4 and shows Suzy Chappell, a woman herself over six feet tall and on the bulky side, rising up over a white fence on her famous mare, Lough Conn Lady. Both creatures have their nostrils flared, eyes slit, hair streaming back, ears close against their heads. Suzy bares her teeth, the muscles in her forearms bulge. The lineaments in the horse's legs above the white rails are sharply etched. John and Anna's neighbors, the Chappells, had scraped together the funds to breed jumping horses, a Connemara and Thoroughbred cross. Connemaras are tough, endurance athletes known for their ability to take fences six feet high. These are ponies that average five feet at the shoulder. Mix that with a steeplechase Thoroughbred and what do you think you get?

"Isn't this just amazing?" says Penny.

"Yes," I say to the new wife, the painting is amazing. "What strikes you about it?"

"Oh, it's just so intense. I can't even imagine how she thought of it."

"The subject? It's—"

"I know where she got the idea, I just don't understand how she knew how to slant it like that, for the impact. It's so crazy."

"But you like it," I say. Lightning spears the far side of the pasture, then the house rattles with the boom. Tina flinches, but I know this house has stood for nearly three hundred years.

"I do like it. I might have hung it somewhere else, because it's unsettling and maybe not everyone wants to deal with it, but I do like to stand here and think about it. Especially knowing the Chappells had to breed those horses on a shoestring the way they did."

After a slight pause, she adds, "Honestly, I'm not sure what John sees in it."

"What do you mean?"

"I think he hung it here so he *wouldn't* have to stumble on it and be startled by it. Right here in the open, he's used to it, it's just a wall decoration. He read a review that said it was good, so it's good, and everyone knows he was married to her. There you go, validated."

I stop looking at the painting, look down at her. She's spoken with no judgment of John that I can detect. I can hear Anna stringing similar sentences together in describing John's approach to art. How bitterly analytical they would sound. If anything, the new wife seems amused.

"Did she ever paint him?" my wife asks.

"Suzy's husband?" Penny says.

"No, John."

"Yes, early on," I tell them. "I don't know where those portraits went. I don't know if she did anything later. After."

"After what?" the new wife says.

"After the divorce. I don't know how much she thinks about John. It's been quite a while. You guys have lived a whole life. Why wouldn't she have lived one as well?"

"But after what?" Penny persists. "What in particular led to that divorce? I can still sense it just walking around some of these rooms." She turns to Tina, as if another woman might know something more.

"I've never met her," Tina says, frowning at me.

"Me either," says the second wife.

That surprises me.

"We read about her, of course," muses Tina.

"I've always had the feeling she didn't just leave," Penny says.

What happened? Tina too had always wanted to know. Did she sleep with someone else? Or, after a third vodka tonic on a particularly thick night on our porch beside the lake, Tina might say: Was it you? Did you sleep with her?

"Did you sleep with Anna?" Tina had repeated, on the drive over. She wasn't accusatory, just curious. We've told each other about our past loves. Sometimes those stories spice up our own sex life. I still find Tina attractive. She's kept her yellow hair yellow, and long. She wasn't going to get the chin-length cut all the other well-groomed women our age tended to wear. "Cutting your hair ages you immediately," she maintains, "turns you into a matron."

It would upset her, though, if I'd slept with Anna and not told her already. That's why she can't let it go. In the end, it would become an accusation, given that I have, after all, failed to introduce her to this painter she's so long admired.

I think of Jimmy Carter and how everyone laughed, because it seemed like such a silly thing to say: "I lusted in my heart." Hasn't everyone? Why confess something so light? On some level Tina, Rosalynn, must know: if he felt compelled to confess, there was nothing light about it. The lust in his heart wasn't anything along the lines of "here she comes just a-walking down the street." It wasn't some coworker he sweated over for six months. It wasn't one of those movies we're automatically loading as we go about the day: the receptionist, the cashier, the buddy's wife, even the son's girlfriend. Beautiful, ordinary, thick, thin, young, old. Even Meryl Streep if that's the movie I'm watching. Bent over the furniture. What was in Carter's heart had to be something dark.

3.

JOHN AND ANNA MET AT COLLEGE, at a suite party we hosted. They were drunk, we were all drunk on Heineken from a keg. I didn't think Anna was anything special at first. Brown hair, brown eyes, medium build. She came with a girl named Susan, whom I noticed more. Susan and I spent all of the weekends and vacations of our junior year together. Not true love, but as close as I cared to come at that point. Of course I've mentioned Susan to my wife.

As for John and Anna, they were inseparable. There's always some couple in college who goes over the edge. When I did catch a glimpse of them, coming out of the laundromat, or sitting in front of the TV in the downstairs common room, they weren't exactly all over each other. There was instead an ease between them. It was like being with two people who went around naked all the time, were so used to it they didn't even know they were naked. You were the weirdo for having your clothes on. God probably felt relieved when Adam and Eve finally ate the apple, went and got their fig leaves.

Anna seemed exotic to most of us because she did not live in a dorm or have any roommates. She had a studio apartment overlooking the Charles and her own scull chained to two hooks under her deck. She took it out at dusk rather than dawn the way most crew people did. Anna wasn't a morning person. She didn't crew. She didn't like team sports. She went for runs and bike rides. When yoga came along she did that. The point was getting out and moving her body so she could think better. That's what she told me the night I got stuck at her apartment in a blizzard. I don't remember why I was there.

"What does an artist need to think about?" I asked. "I'm sorry, I'm not trying to be rude. What you're saying would make more sense to me if you were a poet or a writer, but I would think a painter would be more right-brained, I guess. About your work."

"Some painters and sculptors I know are the opposite of me, they love to get *out* of their heads, as much as possible. But I argue my way through everything I do."

I went out along the hall where she had her paintings stacked and began dragging them into the livingroom light. Most of them were 2x2 or larger. In many of them there did seem to be some kind of dialogue or fight, now that I was looking for it. This was her early work, her art-school work. She was dealing with assignments mostly, bent light on skyscrapers, the same veering light on the scattered trash far below. There was a drawing of all of us in her apartment, nearly passed out from partying, looking not privileged but worn with it, as if we'd already been through our lives and had come round again, were not falling asleep but waking up. I looked at that one for a long time, pretending to be trying to determine which of us was who. It was a rough sketch. There was an oil portrait of John, also falling asleep. One eye still open, looking calm and happy, the other drooping shut, reflecting a lamp in the room and something else, some angry unsettled spirit looming up from a dream about to seize him, you supposed. Seize calm John? Anger, even in a dream?

"How long does it take you to do one of these?"

"That pile's the three and half years I've been here, and some work from some of the summers." There had to be around twenty pieces in her hallway. I tried to imagine staying so productive. Having that much to show for something. I had papers and tests, books I'd read. Most of it was dashed together, destined for the trashcan once I moved on.

"I get stuck on something and I go for a run or a row."

I sipped my Molson, looking at her. Snow was falling hard; the city had shut down. Since we'd first met, her hair had grown out longer. Maybe one of her friends had shown her a different conditioner. It seemed to hold together better. Like most Northeastern intellectual women, she didn't wear much makeup, but she looked more put-together than she had at the party we'd thrown the year before. By now I'd seen it was her eyes—a more uneven color than I'd originally thought—that had captured John's attention; then he'd probably moved on to her body under the baggy Levi's cords and oversized Oxford cloth shirts. For some reason girls of that era felt they had to dress like preppie boys.

"It's misleading, having all this work finished," Anna said.

"What do you mean?"

"I mean I haven't been doing anything else. At least John gets to take a variety of classes at Harvard, even if he isn't paying much attention. I realize he's only going there out of family habit. He should probably go to some business school and be as boring as I am."

I thought the same about John and business school, which is another reason Anna had become attractive to me. The illusion of intimacy that builds through a similarity of insight. "You can't compare art school to business school, Anna."

"No. But it's one-dimensional. It's not as if I get to read great books or study history for balance. There ought to be a general-studies year that they make art students go through. I wish I'd gone to Radcliffe and majored in art. Or Harvard itself. You know it'll be co-ed in another second. They're just being stupid."

"Would you have had as good a pass?"

"Who knows. It's true I've had terrific instructors at the Museum School."

I thought it wonderfully rebellious to go to an art school. A school embedded in a museum, with no compulsory math or science, no foreign language requirement, no humanities, nothing but the One Thing you wanted to do. Anna stole books from me, though, messing with my budget. She probably assumed I could afford them. It's true I was better off than some of our friends, golden as far as room and board went, but with no allowance for personal spending money or socializing. Why else does one send one's son to Harvard if not to socialize? A tic my father had. When I went to sell my books back to the bookstore, there was always something missing. A Dostoyevsky novel, Aristotle's *Poetics*. Then, without ever coming clean, she would give herself away by asking me if I thought plot was ever real or always just a literary device.

"Does it have to be either/or?" I said. "If it's a spy thriller, sure it's device. If it's a story about a marriage, maybe Tolstoy trumped up a few things for dramatic impact." Though if you read Pushkin's biography, or Akhmatova's, you start to realize that the people in those circles did lead lives that sounded pretty crazy: lovers moving in with married couples and then shooting themselves over some other lover who was living with yet another man.

"I don't mean whether dramatic things happen," she said. "I mean the mythos and the pathos, the requirement of reversals and personal change. The ideal that the character should be the one who initiates the reversals and is responsible for them, even if unwittingly. Doesn't Aristotle's instruction that this is how one should create a story suggest that it's how we're to read, also? It's the same in art. You're taught to see a certain way. In fiction there's some sense of causality, but in reality, there's isn't, always."

Or she would say: "Doesn't *pi* bug the shit out of you?"

"Not really. I have a calculator."

"All those constants. They're just shims, you know. To make the math work out. It wouldn't work without them."

"And then what, Anna?"

"And then they'd all be wrong. About the elegance of the universe and all."

"Would the world end?" I said.

"Of course not. But how do they *know* about these constants? They just rush you through it. Oh, just memorize them, you'll be fine, here it is, 2-*pi-r*. But what does that even mean, that this thing you're looking at, holding in your hand if it's a tennis ball, is only an estimate?"

"It's not a very rough estimate."

"It's sloppy work," she said, shaking her head. "It's a loose end. And don't get me started on imaginary numbers. As if the universe is a house of mirrors." She paused. "Maybe it is. What a nightmare."

"I'd think you'd be glad you're not taking math."

"Not really. I like fights."

What the hell was she doing with John, then, the most conflict-avoidant man from the most conflict-avoidant family I'd ever met? In general Wasps are sneaky and understated, but coming from the West I hadn't grasped all the rules yet.

I made a pass at Anna that snowy night at her apartment in college. She let me. Our wool hats and mittens warming on the radiator made the apartment smell like friendly dogs. The beer was sour in our mouths. I brought my hand up under her damp hair, soft and wavy with humidity. I kissed her sharp small nose, her neck. I undid the baggy cardigan sweater. She wore a plain white bra; she'd given the evening no advance thought. A front clasp. Her breasts popped out of it, as beautiful as I'd imagined them. Permanent tan line. She'd grown up on a lake in New York state. She had pointy nipples that were already hard. I kissed them, kissed her mouth, which seemed soft, pulling with something other than desire. Regret, maybe. It made me even more eager. I unzipped her Levi's fly. White cotton underpants. I slid my hand in.

Every time I read one of those thrillers or noir mysteries that describes some young woman with silky pubic hair of some exotic color, I think: what, are you a virgin? In 1972 women had regular pubic hair. It tended to be coarse and dark. *I* was always glad to get my hands on it. Anna lay back on the couch, her breasts bulging out of her sweater. I stood up and unbuckled my belt.

I should never have allowed that much air to pass between us. She sat up as if awakening. "Ethan."

"Please, Anna. Let this be." I knelt beside her and took her face between my hands. I kissed her. She took my tongue. Then she turned her face away.

"Don't say we can't," I said. "It'll make it even worse. Either way we have to go on with things in the morning."

"But—"

"Let wanting be enough," I said. I turned her face back toward mine and kissed her again, pushing her down on the sofa. I was ecstatic with the nudge of her nipples beneath my t-shirt, they were so hard. I reached down and pulled my own fly apart. There was a rippling feeling beneath me, a shudder of warmth and wetness against my neck. I pushed up on my arms. "What's wrong?"

She was crying.

"Anna, what's wrong."

"Look, I'm sorry if I led you on, but I wasn't expecting this. I kissed back because it surprised me and I wanted to see how it felt. And from one kiss we're all the way here, and I don't know how to stop it. You're not listening to me."

One kiss? Talk about the twilight zone. I'd been fantasizing about her for over a year. The one kiss had been a zero-to-sixty dream-car acceleration for me.

"Ethan? I'm going out with your best friend? I shouldn't even be kissing you? Isn't it normal to have a few second thoughts?"

No, silly girl, I was thinking. It's normal to rush right through them as fast as you can. By now she had her boobs wrapped back up in that baggy sweater and her jeans refastened.

I didn't look back on this moment often, but when I did I wondered if I'd done the right thing. I knew what the right answer was, but not what the right *thing* was. That is, what would have happened if I'd wiped the tears from the corners of her eyes with the flat of my thumb, kissed her forehead, then her mouth. And then her nipples again. And then her mouth some more. Maybe pushed a finger inside her. Would it have been too late, then, for her to have stopped?

Or if I'd started later in the night, moved a little slower, talked sweeter.

Would she really have shoved me away? And in the morning would she have been my girlfriend and not John's? It's always there for me, that question. It's a constant regret.

4.

TINA TOO IS A SECOND WIFE, but I don't think of her that way. I was married only briefly the first time, under the influence of a kind of ideal that today makes me cringe. Tina is my wife, the one I'd want to meet again in future lives, if any exist. It is hard for me accept that John probably feels the same way about Penny. That he might see Anna as the juvenile ideal. The true love, versus the real love. This is a conversation I don't want to have with Tina.

Not long ago she brought home a DVD of *Rob Roy*. It's old, but somehow she and her friends had gone on a jag with it. Inspired, no doubt by that *Outlander* series. Liam Neeson, who is on her "list," along with Neil Young. When pressed, I claimed the only celebrity I had the hots for was Gwyneth Paltrow. God, I think she's kind of sniveling, Tina said. God, really?

No, of course not, but was I supposed to say Meryl Streep and Joni Mitchell? In my *fantasy* life? Anyway, she brought *Rob Roy* home so she could show me why she and her friends had loved that movie so much. It's the rape scene, or its aftermath. When Liam is about to go hack his wife's rapist in half with his broadsword (the part I liked), he pauses in the doorway. What shall I name the child? his wife, Mary, asks. In case you don't come back, she means. They don't know who the father is, Rob or the rapist. He pauses, looks her in the eye, says, If it's a girl, call her Mary. If it's a boy, name him Robert Roy MacGregor.

True heroism, my wife said, wet-eyed. She went to get more wine during the sword fight.

You wouldn't want the rapist dead? I said.

I don't know, she said. Maybe.

If it were you? I said.

I don't know. I'd want my husband to say something like that to me, though.

True love? Tina's version. Should it be mine?

There is another Anna piece in John and Penny's livingroom, something smaller, a detail of a dirty, disassembled carburetor. A still life, I guess you could say. Odd, but the choice of hanging makes you look at it for a while. Interesting that John has found this an appropriate subject; but perhaps by now other similar works of hers have found recognition. It is hard at times to find the patterns in his mind.

The new wife has laid out soy cheese and rice crackers along with some Molson beer and a bottle of chardonnay on the side table. None of it looks good. Tina, though, is on her second glass of wine. "So what did happen to her?" my wife asks.

I look at my cell phone. Not that there is a signal, just to check the time. Where is John? Even a record bowel movement can't account for this long of an abandonment. He usually hovers as a host, the scoliosis in his upper back vulturing his neck and head.

"I heard the phone a few minutes ago," Penny says. "There's some kind of mess with something he's up to over on the lake. He's upset about it, I've hardly ever seen anything like it. On top of what happened to the boat. You probably know how smoothly he engineers his deals. He likes everyone coming out happy."

That's true. The last bit of unpleasantness had been his divorce and what had led up to it.

"You know, he still calls Anna from time to time," the new wife says to Tina. "Out of the blue, he'll say, I looked in on Anna the other day, she seems to be doing fine. What am I supposed to say to that? I've asked my friends. Half of them think it's normal to stay friends with an ex, the other half find it shocking." Again she looks at Tina.

"My friends would probably be half and half, too," Tina says. I wonder what kinds of discussions about divorce she's having with her friends. I myself have never contacted my ex, but we parted with very little drama.

"It's normal for John, shocking for what happened," I say.

"Please tell me. Did she have an affair? Did he throw her out? Did his family banish her for some reason?"

"What if it wasn't her?" I say.

"Maybe I'm not starry-eyed," she says.

"You should get the story out of him."

"Ha."

I pick up Anna's saucer from the Chippendale end table. The china was probably about two hundred years old when she'd dug it out of the garden, in a dozen or so pieces. When she washed the dirt away, the blue pattern had been bright as new. It was as if the plate had been thrown in a fit of rage. She'd found every piece. Anna epoxied it together, added a bb pellet, leaving the assembly for guests to tip and tilt as they conversed. It seemed to her a metaphor for the patchwork of the region's history. Now the bullet is missing.

"Is Felix Chappell still around?" I ask. Felix is the stepson of the woman in the horse painting.

"The one they let be sheriff till they found out he was statutory-raping the babysitter?" Penny says.

"Yeah, that one." The babysitter hadn't been the beginning or the end of Felix's raping career.

"He was in and out of jail for many years, then he stayed out of trouble for a while, I think," Penny explains. "Finally he got rearrested for selling coke. Disappeared into the state pen."

We follow her back into the hallway, past a long table loaded with photos of children in athletic poses and prep-school sweatshirts. For all her submissive body language, Penny has managed to get what she's wanted from John. Private elementary school, music lessons, sleep-away camps. These baffled John. It wasn't how he was raised to care for his money. I wonder what John and Anna's once-perfect marriage would have been like if they'd had children together. I think of the clashes Tina and I struggled so hard to work through, Tina hurtling into the our marriage counselor's office, always exactly fifteen minutes late, always a different explanation, fine hair falling out of its braid, blouse cut to hide the D-cups she wished were C-cups, to disguise the ten extra pounds she carried no matter how hard she exercised. We'd debate: how much to intervene when Jensen's grades dropped. Whether we should crack down on the kids' pot-smoking or assume that because we survived, they would. At what point to provide a car, and what kind. It takes time, it takes matters like these, to test a marriage.

"I was thinking I'd just start laying out the meal, since he's being so rude," Penny says. "Would you mind helping me set it up? Then I'll go get him."

I had stopped in the hallway, so surprised by my thought that John and Anna's marriage might have run aground later. This is not to say that what happened saved any greater pain. That would be hard to imagine. But my pain over watching what I used to think of as an ideal marriage fail, the cynicism that arose in me over whether people could love. That was unnecessary, as cynicism perhaps always is. That is to say, the marriage was never ideal, it was just me who dreamed it so.

Funny the peace age brings to you. I wasn't ready for this insight when their marriage did fail; now I don't really care. I had wound up feeling perhaps twice as disillusioned with John as I might have felt had his marriage simply run out of steam a bit later.

I follow Penny onto the glassed porch where the table is already laid. Rain ticking on the metal roof. The nice silver, the regular dishes. One leaf extended, the other dropped. Placemats rather than a cloth, to expose the fine wood. An arrangement of autumn leaves, simple blown-glass candlesticks. Red wine opened to breathe but left in its bottle. Scotch, a dewy pitcher of water, no ice.

"Why don't you let me haul him out of there," I say.

I walk toward John's study. I can hear him on the phone. He's talking very quietly and firmly. I'd heard him like this a few times. Usually it had involved the Chappells in one way or another. One of Suzy's horses had got loose and crashed itself into John's daughter's Jetta. The horse got up and ran off. It seemed to be fine. The Jetta had $1200 in damage, which John could well afford. Unlike the Chappells, who always seemed to be struggling, despite the horse breeding, gravel hauling, logging operations. Who probably didn't have whatever kind of insurance would cover a horse crashing into someone's car. The Chappells should have taken better care of their fence. John got on the phone and made the point very clear in that soothing voice of his. "Is the horse okay? Wonderful. I'm glad the horse is okay. And I'm glad my daughter is okay. That's wonderful, too. It could have been so much worse. But my daughter's car is not okay. She needs her car to drive to school and to her job after sports. She needs it by next Monday. The car is going into the shop today. It will be done Friday. Please stop by Herman's and pay for it then."

As lightning moves off the Ridge and down into the Merrimack River valley, there's a final saluting boom. The power fails. John's call truncates. "I said—" he says.

For some reason I grope my way back down the hall instead of knocking on the office door.

The horse vs. Jetta call had been years ago. It seems unlikely that the call I overheard now would involve the Chappells.

5.

SUZY CHAPPELL HAD LOST her prized brood mare, the one in the livingroom painting, in 1978. A terrible accident. A year later, Anna Halloran was using binoculars to watch Suzy dismantle her steeplechase course. You could call it spying. Probably a lot of people in the village would if they knew she was doing it. It was research if you understood Anna's mind. It didn't matter anyway because I was probably the only one who knew exactly what she was doing. John was at his office during the day. Sometimes I would be heading in or out to work or school while Anna was looking across at the meadows on Ranger Mountain. I would go and stand beside her, try to make her describe the way images went into her head.

"I wouldn't be able to do this if you hadn't spent last summer working over there," she had said. The previous year I'd skidded logs for Rusty Chappell, which had enabled me to earn the Perkinses' nominal rent plus book and gas money—my parents still didn't cover personal expenses related to my schooling—and to bring back stories of local life to Anna.

"I don't get that," I said. "Why can't you just paint what you see? How does it help if I tell you a story about it? That seems pretty verbal."

"Why shouldn't I be verbal?"

I'd said, "I don't know. It goes back to what we talked about in school, I guess, where I kept thinking art school should be enough."

"Well, it wasn't. Anyway, the things you told me about the people in the village make what I do feel more dynamic. There's more tension in the work."

"Then I'm glad."

"That's why I told you."

"Are you glad you're here?" I asked. "Way up here in the woods like this? You don't get out much."

Anna twisted her mouth. "Can't say yes, can't say no. Right now there's material."

I knew she was in a tricky position. She had no money of her own, and I assumed there was a deal between her and John—some agreement he'd made to support her as an artist. When I asked her, once, she said only: He buys me horses to paint.

Do you want to paint them?

No, but as you know there are other things around here to paint. Also, things I think about while looking at horses.

What kinds of things?

How parts fit together, how life moves. How large creatures with poor eyesight find their footing, or lose it.

It didn't occur to me then to ask about friends, her social life. She'd had friends in college, at least a few. Now I look at women around me, Tina with her beloved Pietra, other women I know, and of course they have many other female friends. They're *always talking*. Sometimes they talk to me, but first they talk to one another. If they think their husband is having an affair, they discuss all the signs. If they think he should get a vasectomy, they find out from their friends how it works. If they want to make a career move, they call up a dozen people who have done something similar. It's amazing the database any woman can access with the help of a cellphone contact button. During the two years I lived on Perkins Ridge, I saw maybe four people visit Anna. She might have gone over to Lansing to meet up with a local artist a few times.

Her busyness obscured any loneliness. Maybe she didn't notice her loneliness, either. Though I sensed my questions were interruptive, I was curious about her seeing, so I made a point of bothering her. There was another question that hung between us, or I thought it did. I liked to think of it hanging there. It went back to those early days in college, the night of the blizzard especially. Not a big deal; we were all adults now. That night in her apartment gave a bit of what I saw as enjoyable tension to our time together.

One day, I came hurrying out to my car. I was running late. I only paused when I heard Anna cry. Caught up in her observations, she had tripped, snapped her ankle. Struck her head on a rock. She was gushing blood at the temple. Although she could sit up, she was disoriented, the binoculars cracked, hanging from her shoulder. She kept pushing at the air with one of her hands, the way a mime sometimes presses at a fake wall. She did this at an angle, as if the invisible wall or ceiling were bearing down on her. Because of the blood and possible concussion I called the emergency line. Otherwise I would have loaded her into my Saab and driven her over to the hospital in Lansing. I called the sheriff, then I called John, who did not answer in his office. His father's secretary had retired. John hadn't wanted the expense of taking on another. I think he felt young still, thought of a secretary as something an older man would have.

I left it for the sheriff's dispatch to order the ambulance. I made a quick call to the professor I was interning with that summer. I left a notice that I would probably not show up for my research commitment that day.

Because I called dispatch, Sheriff Felix Chappell came up Perkins Ridge. That he was the sheriff was laughable, and a function of a certain kind of good-old-boy network in Enshaw. He encountered Anna half-lying on the ground, bleeding, in pain. He came to know that she would often be home alone, absorbed in her work, while her husband was at an office miles away, not answering his phone.

Felix should have called the ambulance. I knew this, but he was the sheriff. I didn't stop him from wrapping Anna's head in a towel, loading her with her broken leg and her probable concussion into the back of his cruiser, driving her to the hospital in Lansing himself. Perhaps my wits were dulled—I hadn't been sleeping well because one of the horses often bashed around in his stall. I followed in my Saab after another unsuccessful attempt to reach John. The hospital staff, knowing Anna was a Perkins, whisked her to a private area. Using the white phone in the waiting room, I was finally able to let John know what was going on. I said the sheriff was helping us out. "I'll be right over," said John.

I thought Felix would move on by now, needing to get back to dispatch or go hide his car somewhere in the middle of nowhere, in case someone went speeding by in an unreasonably slow zone. Instead, he sat in the waiting room, legs out, hat in the lap, as if he were actually worried.

"What's he doing here?" John wanted to know, as soon as we got past the waiting room and down the hall toward where they had Anna. I explained the chain of events. John did not like it. I could see there was not going to be any way to make it come clear in his mind. How Anna had fallen, why I had called dispatch, why an ambulance had never been sent, why Felix Chappell was sitting in the waiting room. With John's confusion as a guide, a person could readily become disoriented himself.

We reached Anna's room. Both of us entered. John hesitated in the doorway while I unthinkingly went straight up to the bedside. She was semi-awake, staring woozily out the window. "Anna, we found John. He's here now."

That seemed to hook John into the room. He pulled up a chair and bent over her, his big hands stroking her hair away from the bandage. She turned toward him. I made myself leave. The tenderness between them, the way her eyes lit when she saw him, excluded me.

Did I want her, or did I want what they had? Was there any difference?

The next time the cruiser came up the hill to the house I didn't think much of it. East Enshaw was a small village. It wasn't unlikely for the Perkinses to be of special concern. Anna was on crutches, swinging to her studio daily, if on shortened hours due to headaches. I was pulling out of my parking spot. Anna gave Felix a tight little smile and a finger wave, without really lifting her hand from the crutch. I maneuvered my car alongside her. "Do you need anything? Do you want me to stay for a bit?"

"Not that I can think of," she said. "Should be all right."

"He's supposed to be a jerk." Felix's biological father, whom I'd worked for, was a headstrong enough man. Felix had been raised by his mother's second husband, who could ruin any child.

Having pulled into my spot, Felix got out of the car. He had a way of carrying himself. Not a swagger like Rusty's, but a physical mastery all the same. Felix Chappell was a redhead, darker than his father, and not freckled or fair. Where his father was built like a linebacker, Felix was rangy, his muscles ropy. Strong, though. Physically, I was no match for either man. Neither was John, who was skinny, had that issue with his neck.

"What's he going to do?" Anna said. "Attack me here in my home? He'd have to kill me. Even if you leave you'd still be a witness. You'd be the relentless hero tracking him down. I have every faith."

"Gee, thanks."

It turned out he had some form he needed her to sign. It seemed on the up and up. I did drive off.

I didn't see Anna until the next day. She'd banged her ankle on a stair. She didn't seem interested in talking about Felix. A week later, he came again. I didn't know he was there until I came down from my apartment. Felix had parked behind my car. He'd dragged a lawn chair over by the studio and stretched himself out. I went over and knocked on Anna's door. She unlocked it and I entered. She looked pale and grim.

"What the hell?" I said.

She shook her head. "I told him I was busy. He doesn't have any forms or anything. He says he's off work, just wanted to check on me. I need to pee but I'm not going out there. I think I'll pee in a can."

"That's ridiculous. It's your own home. Ask him to leave."

"I did."

"Call John."

"I'd have to go past him into the house to do that."

"All right, I will. Are you afraid of him?"

"Not exactly. I just don't want to deal with him. Look what I'm in the middle of." The painting was a strangely distorted view from what might have been the backseat of a cop car. The driver had red hair. A painting is of course two-dimensional, but this one gave you the feeling that you were actually stuck inside the painting, that you, the viewer, were also living in a two-dimensional world. I remembered how Anna had seemed to press against a ceiling after she had hit her head. This effect in the painting was interesting, but also there was a range of light coming in through both sides of the car that gave a sense of motion, of hurry.

"Do you need to get to class?" she asked.

"No, I was just going up to the library to study," I said. "It's Saturday. Probably why he's off. I'll distract him for you."

I stepped out of the studio. "Want a beer?" I said to Felix.

"Sure." He peered around me. He couldn't see Anna through the clouds reflected in the glass.

I went into the main kitchen and called John. No answer. I grabbed two Molsons out of the fridge.

"Hopin for a Bud or a Rollin Rock."

"None of that up here," I said.

"Snobs, ay."

"Some ways," I said.

"She stay busy in there all day long, even she's hurt like that?"

"She works as hard as anyone I know," I said.

"Won't take a beer or nothin. On a Sat'r'day?"

"John's off working, right? She'd be working, too."

Felix shook his head. He was out of uniform, wearing Wrangler jeans, tan work boots made in a defunct factory along the Sugar River, and a white T-shirt, tucked in. All extremely clean.

He'd have to kill me, Anna had said the previous week. I studied his flat brown eyes as they studied the Molson label. I wasn't sure Felix Chappell would have teased Anna's logic all the way out.

He said, "You can see a lot from up here. Lay of the land. What Old Rusty's up to. I could sit up here and mark down the speeders till kingdom come. When kingdom come I could go down, spend one day catchin just the ones I marked. I guess that's power, ay? Sittin up here looking down on the world. But John got better things to do somewheres else." He shot a look at the blank studio windows and shook his head again.

"John," I said, "has plenty to do."

"Mind if I use the can?" he asked.

"Go right ahead."

I followed him into the house. I wanted to get a little food. I called John again and got through. While Felix was in the bathroom, I explained to John what was happening. I shouldn't say I explained, because John was mystified as to why Felix Chappell should be up on Perkins Ridge on a Saturday for no reason. However, I was able to communicate that it was he, John, who was going to have to come home, soon, and get Felix Chappell to leave.

"Nice place," Felix said, joining me in the kitchen. He turned around, looking at the counters and cabinets, the double ovens and the special grill built into the island. All the copper pots and pans hanging from the ceiling. It wasn't what you saw every day in East Enshaw at that time, that's for sure. Most people, even wealthier families in the larger, better-built

Colonials, still had painted white plywood cabinets and Formica counters. They had stainless sinks and a single, long fluorescent light fixture in the center of the ceiling. Maybe another one over the sink. Some used a variety of antique hutches and tables for food preparation.

What are you thinking, Bud? I wondered. You have to know this isn't for you. There are some things a sheriff can get away with and some he cannot.

Felix walked over to the bay window in the breakfast area. "Anyone ride that horse over there?"

"Which horse?"

"The one penned in that smaller fence, there." He pointed. John and Anna kept a gray horse apart from the other two. The one who kept me awake with his bashing.

"He bites, I think. Or kicks."

"She don't ride?"

"She paints them." She didn't, though. Traditional New England scenes no longer interested her. She had begun instead to focus on an underside: emptied fabric mills, machinery rusting in weeds, cellarholes deep in the woods, an abandoned gun factory, and, still unfinished, a steamer that had sunk a century ago in Big Shire Lake. Divers had never found the wreck in the lake's murk, but Anna had dug up drawings and photographs of similar boats. She'd snorkeled around the possible site, swimming as deep as she dared, to get a sense of the light. "The boulders down there," she'd said, "are spooky. Ship-sized."

"That horse," Felix said, pointing. "He shouldn't be alone like that."

"What do you mean?"

"Can't you see? Look how he's pacin. Pacin and pacin."

"Jaybird. He's like that." As we watched, Jaybird went over and leaned against the fence, whinnying at the other horses, who ignored him. He bit the white boards, then kicked them, turning with a half-rear to trot the circle inside the small square.

"He's chewed up all his grass," Felix observed.

"I'm sure he gets the recommended amount of hay and grain."

"Maybe he does. If he don't like the other horses, get him a goat. You tell em. Anna and John, get him a pony or a goat. That horse has a brain going in circles faster than he can run. He'll run himself right out of his head." Felix looked around the kitchen again. "Looks like they can afford a damn goat."

John was home before Felix finished his second beer. I couldn't help but be impressed with how things were handled. John drove up, parked his workaday Blazer in the barn. He stepped into Anna's studio for about two minutes, then ambled over to the house. John had a funny way of walking. I suppose he had slightly dysplastic hips; Anna said the roll he used in compensation was swashbuckling, sexy. His father, now living, in a shocking break in character, in Bermuda, walked the same way. I wouldn't quite call it swashbuckling myself, because otherwise John was so reserved, and because of the shoulder hunch. Still, when he entered the house, where Felix and I had remained, there was no question whose territory it was.

"Nice of you to drop by, Felix," he said. He went to the fridge and cracked his own beer. "Rare pleasure."

"Was in the neighborhood."

John nodded. There was no other neighborhood. "Thanks for your help the other day. Anna's doing fine."

"What I'm here for. She don't come out of that studio or office or whatever you call it, does she. She stops for no man."

"Not even me," John said, "as you can see. Not much point in stopping in for a friendly visit when someone's trying to get work done around here."

"Perkinses been that way for more than two hundred years, they say."

"They do say."

"Guess you went and married one of your own kind."

John laughed. "My mother wasn't convinced at first. But if she could see Anna now. Here, let me take that." John smoothly cleared away all the bottles, including my own, and neatened up the counters. He checked his watch.

Felix surprised me by taking the hint without any sign of rancor. "Glad it all worked out. You know who to call, you need any kind of help." He drew that word out, looking both of us in the face before he was done saying it. He strode over to his cruiser without even glancing at the studio, got in, drove off. He tapped the horn once, in a friendly way.

"Any kind of hel-puh?" I said to John.

"Any kind at all."

"Could I grow sinsi in the chicken coop? I'll cover my tuition and get myself out from under the thumb of Uncle Brock and my dad."

"Uh, no."

"Darn."

Then John said, "There's tons of acres way up on Baldy where you could grow it. More work, but bigger yield, less risk. Easy to keep people off it. It's always been Perkins land. My mother was vigilant about trespassers. You don't need the signoff from the sheriff for that."

My comment had been three-quarters in jest. The little lost quarter was rolling on home. "I'd need sheds, though."

"Some up there. Stone cottages, might need fixing. It's all old meadows, so there are sheep and cow tenders' shacks. Grown back to forest mostly, but still some open field. No one will catch it unless they fly right over."

I realized he'd been thinking about this for a while. Maybe it was even why he'd agreed to let me stay here. John was a prude in some ways, but not when it came to a good business proposition. There were several proprietorships—a couple of the better restaurants, for example—over in

Lansing that had been launched with money earned from a few smuggling trips in the Caribbean. "Going sailing," a chef might say, when he wanted to raise the funds for his own place. I understood, because John had told me, that it had started with a son of one of Lansing's leading families. A friend of John's before boarding school. Sometimes that friend's mother got confused as to which of her children was the more successful—the drug lord or the second son, who'd stayed out of all that, but who'd never grown rich. It hadn't escaped John that his own parents enjoyed frequenting the restaurants that opened up after the sailing trips. Unlike the restaurateurs, John did have inheritance. He already had good business sense and asset management. He didn't need to add illegal activities and their risks to his portfolio.

But land is not a liquid asset. Under-the-table cash never hurts any operation.

"You serious?" I said.

"We could hike up and check it out."

"Right now?" It looked like he was getting ready to change his shoes.

"Sure, why not? I'm home early. Like the sheriff said, Anna's not about to stop for anybody."

We started on an old cow trail and wound our way along mossy, collapsing stone walls. The ridge steepened immediately, leading toward Bald Peak. There were only so many names you could come up with; every mountain around had a glaciated granite crown, even if not as bulging as Ranger's. I noticed that every five or ten minutes a trail—sometimes a wagon track, and sometimes just a game or sheep trail—would delve off into the woods. After about half an hour, John touched my arm. We turned left, toward the south-facing side of the ridge.

"That Felix," I said. "He's something else."

John sidled around a rock in the path. "Long story, like everything around here. I went to grade school in the Harbor, you know."

I didn't know, but I supposed in rural places like this, you sent your kids to public school, perhaps off to boarding school later.

"It was—still is—a two-room school. Felix was in fifth grade when I was in third, so we had the same teacher." John shook his head. "As dumb as some of you guys made me feel at Harvard, Felix made me feel like a genius. I think he'd stayed back a hundred times already. I'd help him with his spelling. You can guess how mad that made him, skinny little third-grade twerp like me."

"Not being able to spell doesn't make a person dumb."

"No, but at some point you have to sit yourself down and concentrate. There were a lot of kids who had trouble sitting still, but he was the worst of them. He made it hard for everyone. He was always going on about snobs on the hill, wanting to come up and see, come up and play." John stopped hiking, gestured down toward East Enshaw. "*I* was always down in the village playing. That's where all the kids were. We'd ride bikes, jump in the brook, skate on the pond. I'd go out of my mind sometimes as an only child up here."

"Was Felix down there, too?"

"Not after his mom married a Shattuck. They'd come down to swim at the lake and people would clear away. It was always believed that they had lice or scabies. That's what went around at school. I hated having to work with Felix on spelling, afraid I'd catch something. Also you never knew what a Shattuck would do. Felix wasn't so bad. But his next-down half-brother? One day he just hurled a huge padlock, size of a fist, right at the blackboard. Went whizzing by my left ear, nearly hit Mrs. Cole's shoulder.

"God," I said, stepping around John to pick up the pace.

"Just a thug family."

"If everyone hated them so much, how did he make Sheriff?" I knew it was still the case that all the Shattucks were seen as bad news.

"Don't know. He's not a Shattuck in the end, mainly. My parents didn't block it. Mom was sick already. My father was thinking more and more about Bermuda. He wasn't paying attention to the community so much." I could hear the disapprobation, mixed almost with wonder, in John's voice. *Could* you cease your involvement in local affairs? How unexpected of his father.

The trail initially led through a mixture of evergreen and birch, but soon it opened up into a gently sloping meadow full of wild strawberries. It wasn't large. There were maple and birch saplings scattered about, some poplar. A few pine trees about waist height coming up. Moss underfoot testified to moisture retention. "Wow," I said. "This is perfect."

"There are more like this, but I thought it would be enough for a start."

"Yup." We'd want to know how intense a strain we could breed in these conditions. How it all worked. I'd never done this, but I figured it wasn't rocket science.

John led me through the meadow to show me an old stone building nestled into the corner of the field, where the rock walls came together. The building had been well mortared. It needed very little work, just a bit of metal for the roof. It had no windows. I thought we could put a couple of solar panels on the thing to run some lights inside. Nerves rippled into the center of my body. We might really do it. Break the law on a grand scale. Become felons. When I looked at John calmly surveying his land, I relaxed. The risk would have to be manageable or he wouldn't consider it. Who around here was going to run a bust on Perkins property?

John whistled most of the way down, a Jonathan Edwards tune. We shared a bowl, the long-handled mahogany piece he'd had since at least freshman year, and my bud. Finally he told me why he was interested in this venture. He wanted to have children. Anna did too, but she was worried about her work. They'd arrived at a deal: hire a nanny parttime, but this would be an added expense, one he didn't want to cover out of *his* business proceeds. Even if he could afford it. It was some kind of principle. Wives worked nowadays, they contributed.

John Perkins had then, still has now, a real estate development firm in Lansing, where he mostly sold or developed some of the land that had been in his family since before the Revolution. The grant from Governor Wentworth in fact hung framed in the foyer of his house. It was the founding grant for the towne of End Shire, out of which John's family had carved East End Shire, then sliced off a portion extending all the way down to Newford in the south and east, all the way up to what was now Enshaw Harbor in the north and west, circling around to the richer town of Lansing. It had all been first-come, first served back then, when New Hampshire had just separated from Massachusetts. New Hampshire and New York squabbling over what would emerge as Vermont. The Perkinses were grabbing land from the newly defeated French. Then, during the Revolution, out of the hands of Tories.

They'd been Tories, themselves, John admitted to me, back at Harvard, switching at the last minute. Luckily, he said. They took the properties of their friends, I surmised.

Sure, he told me as we hiked back down Baldy, Anna worked hard, but one never knew with art. It might never pay off. "I'm not sure about this shift in her subjects," he said.

"Moving away from the landscapes?" I'd never thought she was that serious about pretty pictures. She wasn't doing anything like that in art school, so I figured the landscape thing would pass.

"This new stuff seems bizarre. What would you call it, 'rural industrialism?'"

"That's not bad. Maybe industrial pastoralism."

"Whatever. It seems risky."

"Moving up here was pretty risky, when you think about it," I said. John stopped on the trail below me, swinging around.

"Come on, John. Being away from all her connections, the galleries, the big critics? Her work needs an edge if she's going to find a way back in. If she's not going to be just another painter with a booth full of pretty scenes at the Craftsman's Fair."

He looked at me in the dim forest light, then took another hit. "Oh," he said. A surprised sort of oh. Then, "huh." I guessed that he had indeed pictured her showing her work at the Fair. He would have been proud. If she had her paintings hanging in one of the banks over in Lansing.

"Nothing against the Fair," I said. "I've bought maybe six or seven wedding presents there myself." We started down again.

"I grew up going to it every year," John said. "People come from all over New England. It's a great way to get discovered. Some of the exhibitors are major New York artists with summer homes on the lake."

"Right," I said. I knew Anna was planning to show. "I just think she's looking for more than just selling some of her work, you know? Down the road, I mean. After going to that school, she might be thinking big."

"I went to Harvard and was happy to come home."

I raised my palm. "It's beautiful here, that's for sure."

"Beauty is what an artist needs," said John. He frowned, bringing his eyebrows together over his nose. "She has that, all day, everyday. That should be enough, right? Shouldn't it? The ability to do her work all day, every day?"

"Sure," I said. I was certain that this had been part of the promise of their marriage for Anna. This, and the spark I had always seen between them, those early years at school.

We've had lifetimes together, Anna had told me.

You believe that stuff? You don't even believe in *pi*.

She said, I dreamed I was in a house with John, only it wasn't John, it was like some Amish guy, or some Puritan guy, big and burley, in a black suit. Long black beard. Looked nothing like our John with his sandy thinning hair. Nothing like him. Totally was him. The house was white and bright with big windows and no curtains. Old panes, you know, big tall rectangular windows. A long hall. A foyer, yellow paint, a settee, dark blue. I was pregnant, and he was kneeling before me. I had a print dress, he had his hands, huge hands, on my belly. He was praying. He was so devout. I was not a member of the community, whatever it was, but I respected it, and I loved him.

She'd said it—I loved him—desolately, describing the dream, when I came for their wedding at twenty-five, as if she had no hope of ever explaining it to me.

When John and I got back down off Baldy, Anna had left her studio and come into the main house. She had water heating in a big pasta pot, an expensive-looking jar of spaghetti sauce standing on the maple counter. Broccoli chopped and sitting beside the steamer. She was seated at the kitchen table with her leg propped on a chair and a bag of frozen peas stuffed into the top of the cast.

"That's as good as it gets, guys," she said. "Ethan, you're invited to dinner if you boil the pasta and do the dishes."

"Here, I'll help," John said, helpfully. He put the vegetables in the steamer and then sat down.

"Thanks, man." I said.

He giggled.

"You're stoned," Anna said. She rolled her eyes. John brought his eyebrows together. Most of the time she had seemed too preoccupied with her own work to notice our partying.

I poured some chablis. "It was a fantastic hike," I said. "I forgot everything you could see from up on Old Baldy."

"But not the lake," she said.

"Not Shire. Todd Pond was looking nice and blue, though, not so muddy." I had only noticed this in passing, I'd been so absorbed in dreaming up a business plan. I really wanted to come out of business school without any loans.

"They should dredge that pond," Anna said. "Get a good channel running into the Gillingham Fen, and see if some of those mosquitos wouldn't clear out."

"Why would they dredge it?" John said, shrugging. "Those cottages aren't worth enough."

"Chicken or egg, I guess," Anna replied. "Real estate might go up over there if the lakes were nicer."

John didn't respond. His holdings were all on Big and Little Shire Lakes, sure to be popular with the folks from Boston, Providence, Manhattan until the apocalypse. He had no reason to think about the smaller camps on the smaller lakes for the smaller people. But I kept it in mind. Not the dredging, that would be too much of a project. The idea that you could pick up cottages on some of these littler lakes for cheap, still, that eventually there'd be people who just wanted a place within a couple of hours of Boston. They might be like me, transplanted to the financial centers on the East Coast, unaware of the unstated requirement to spend your summers on the same lake where your friends' families had been vacationing for two hundred years. Let the tattered remnants of the old-money crowd chug around Big Shire Lake with their Chris-Crafts. Most people could be happy on a smaller lake with a Starcraft. Maybe with the proceeds from my operation I could buy a little camp on Todd or Otter Pond and flip it. I'd only need to do a couple. I didn't need to get in on John's territory.

We ate right in the kitchen, to spare having to truck back and forth with the dishes, with Anna and her leg.

"K, guys," Anna said. "Thanks for the help. I'm heading straight to bed."

She did look pale. "Does it hurt?" I asked.

"I'm surprised. I've never broken a bone before," she said. "Also my head is killing me. It's been a nightmare to focus all day. I hardly got anything done."

It occurred to me later that it had never occurred to me then to ask her what Felix had said to her, either during the ride to the hospital, or when he'd attempted to check on her later. It had all been distanced by the peaceful stroll through the woods. She went up the stairs, one at a time, using the crutches slowly but skillfully.

"Could you help me get set up with a water glass and a book and all that?" she called back down.

I nearly started after her but checked myself. John kept rinsing the dishes. Only under my stare did he seem to understand that she had been talking to him. I finished the dishes and went out to my own apartment. The night was thick with heat and fireflies. I thought about smoking a little more pot, but I had to work for my professor the next day, early. I read a little of the professor's draft manuscript regarding risk-taking behaviors among fund managers. Sooner or later this would be my life for real. In 1979, when you'd had a trust fund, however small, you might see investment management as an inevitable career, but if you'd also spent some time following the Grateful Dead, you might not really understand, in your bones, that it was going to happen. Working on Wall Street was as abstract as getting arthritis. Childbirth, I'm told, is like this too. People try to warn women, but they put off being convinced.

From the other part of the barn, I could hear the horses, mostly Jaybird kicking at the walls. I reminded myself to mention Felix's comment to John or Anna the next day. Now that Felix had mentioned it, I was troubled by the horse's isolation.

6.

I LEFT THE HOUSE WHEN JOHN DID, around seven the next morning, following his Blazer down the hill. We both took 107 for a ways, but I got on the interstate and accelerated toward Hanover. I never looked forward to my job, but once I stepped into my professor's office and began working with the material, I always got lost in it. In many ways it was no different from skidding logs with Rusty Chappell, or teaching sailing, or, probably, learning to grow sinsemilla. Some jobs were more pleasurable because you were moving your body, you had the feel of the air and sun on your skin, but others were fun because of the way they used up more of your mind. In all cases and for different reasons you tended to slip into a kind of trance until the problem at hand was resolved. I'd been going to the library and gathering information for Dr. Banson, a trim, goateed fellow with a bit of a slouch. I hadn't known his sort existed when I was an undergraduate in liberal arts. The physical type I recognized, but the intellectual category seemed strange. He was doing serious research in the School of Business, as if it were an actual discipline.

When I found what he needed in the library, I photocopied articles for his files. That part hadn't been too interesting. After that I had begun distilling the points that were relevant to Banson's argument about risk onto index cards, which I was storing in a recipe box divided by topic and appropriately cross-referenced for the bibliography I was also building.

He was still working on a typewriter, which may have accounted for his hunch. The personal computer would not become commonly used for another few years, and even then many students would go to computer labs to write up their papers, inserting five-inch floppy disks into DOS machines with cathode-ray tube monitors, sitting in rows elbow-to-elbow in the middle of the night. For that short period of time, there was something strangely communal about the experience of writing a paper.

At this time, of course, all the studies and writers of articles were still focused on male risk-taking and fund management. It was thought that most of the past behaviors had been too conservative. Funds were run by men still traumatized by the memories of the Depression. As a result, even when the market went up, many prestigious funds lost money or held steady, while younger beneficiaries, often powerless to change the terms of the trust management, seethed, looking for ways to sue. My professor was writing about how to select managers so as to optimize for calculated risk management while screening out the most irresponsible types. It seemed he was going to argue that you still wanted men of the finest educational backgrounds, with solid socialization and good networks. But a little flair—some time spent outside the office skydiving or skiing in the Alps—would be a good sign. What about a background in pot farming? I felt like asking. I'd looked over Dr. Banson's shoulder when I'd set down the last box of index cards. "The key is in where the <u>commitments</u> lie," he'd typed.

"What does that mean, exactly?" I'd asked, and he'd jumped. He spun his stool around, annoyed.

I took two steps back but asked again. "Do you mean that a good investment manager is all-in with the risks, like a rock-climber who can fully commit to the next move even though it may kill him, or that he's anchored to the real world somehow by his commitments? Like, he's committed to an ethical system, or to a community, or something like that?"

"We should go for a drink, Codding. We've never done that, have we? In the meantime, look. These guys like flying under the radar. They like secrecy. They're good at trends. They like going against conventional wisdom. All of this gives you a big head. So what keeps them from making a mistake? Two things. Having skin in the game, enough to make a difference. Also shame. Having external commitments that they'd lose face in front of if they screw up big."

"So you're saying both kinds of commitment."

"Yes, I am."

"Thank you, Dr. Banson. Please put that in your paper. It will make it stronger."

He regarded me for a moment, then smiled and turned back to his typewriter.

As I drove home in the evening, I began speeding. This was always risky behavior in New Hampshire. The cops had nothing better to do. Despite the lack of taxation in that state, they had an awful lot of cops. Sometimes they would even use police officers as flag boys on construction projects. I turned up on the volume on the eight-track, but that didn't soothe my agitation. Although not the Targa, the Saab didn't really mind the speed, not on the Interstate. I was hungry, also worried for some reason. I kept turning over the facts I'd been jotting down for Banson. I thought about pot growing. It seemed a measured risk, but of course many men wouldn't take it. John was a man averse to risk, I'd always believed. A fair-weather sports-car driver, someone who took his attractive but unpredictable wife out and about only on Sundays. Nevertheless, he was *committed.* He'd married Anna. He was committed to his family history, to the estate, to the area surrounding the lake, to conserving and increasing his family's assets. But look what he was willing to do. Not just by investing in my small operation, but also by selling off some of the holdings that had been in the family since the original grant from Benning Wentworth—essentially from King George II. Even his father hadn't been so bold. John Perkins Senior number whatever had invested in other concerns, but never real estate development. Never the real stuff, never so close to home. John tended to look at things differently: I have this, I want that. I'll use this to get that. What did he want, though? Why?

The research I was examining said there was no reason. Just the thrill of getting. If John were smarter, quicker, he could have gone to Wall Street himself. Here on Perkins Ridge, in a small pond like Lansing, the fact that he had always been a beat behind the Harvard conversation didn't register. On Big Shire Lake among the Manhattanites and Bostonians who had been summer people for ages, he was known and respected. Considered thoughtful and classy rather than slow. He could have his thrill in this environment. A calculated risk among his moneyed clients could pay off big. Yet failure would bring plenty of shame.

I wondered about my own self, getting into a higher-stakes world, dealing in pot, eventually flipping houses, trading stock, when I didn't know why I was there. By birthright like the rest of them, I supposed, but did I have that same gene, the thing that made you like it for the rush, whatever it was that made skiers ski and skydivers plunge?

I'd come close to pushing things only twice in my life, really. The second time had been working for Rusty Chappell the previous summer, skidding logs and just generally hanging out with a rougher class of people than I was used to. I'd been over my head and thrilled by that. In a way I'd fed off the darkness that afflicted their lives, knowing that I could go safely back to mine. Or believing so. And so I had. The first time had been that night back in college when I got trapped by the snow in Anna's apartment.

She'd given me so little to go on. Her face unreadable. People's faces at that age and in New England so often were. Life was a poker game, even when there was nothing to win. Everyone was damned if they were ever going to give away a feeling. Some of my Colorado ranching relatives were guarded with their emotions, but that didn't come from caginess or dishonesty. When I came East for prep school I often felt as if I'd been beamed down onto an alien planet populated by Heinlein's Martian rocks or some kind of insect. Why? you wondered. Why were New Englanders like this? What had been done to them?

Anna put her feelings onto her canvases. As I've already said, she wasn't as well read as the Radcliffe girls, though she tried to catch up. Probably nothing can make up for having that material driven into you during those key developmental years in a good prep school. Still, her conversation was interesting, what she *saw* was interesting. I had two or three other girlfriends. I slept with them. I bought them presents. I met the parents of at least one of them. But I never thought too seriously about them, I don't believe, now, looking back.

I wasn't just fantasizing sexually about Anna back then. I finished conversations in my mind. Considered things I should have said, more eloquent comebacks. Further thoughts on mathematical constants. I stopped at Faneuil Hall, I bought treats for her that I later went home and ate myself. One Memorial Day I was caught unawares while a small parade marched by. Several bands preceded by scout troops with their proud mothers. I wondered if these parents really thought scouting so harmless. It was *Memorial* Day, honoring dead troops, and here were these scouts, which if you think about it are pre-troops. Is this what you really want to get your sons psyched up for? Aren't the scouts kind of like the Komsomol? Discuss.

This was the kind of conversation Anna and I might have had. During the time I waited for the parade to pass, I ached to have her at my side, ached physically. I couldn't imagine I'd ever have a mate I'd be able to turn to so instinctively to share those kinds of thoughts with. I also couldn't imagine that she and John ever had those kinds of conversations. Komsomol? John Perkins?

John Perkins making love with Anna Halloran. The mind veered. He was awkward in that aristocratic way the inbred often are. Look at the royal family. They manage to pull it off and turn it into something that they're even snobby about. Oh, my huge ears and incredibly ugly nose? These go back to William the Conqueror. My sinuses that produce buckets of snot, my migraines that put me out of commission for days on end, well. Genetic, you know. Everyone in my family has bad breath. Shrug. We're all terrible sleepers. We have to bring these white noise machines when we travel.

And we all went around mad about him. At first I thought his extraordinary taste, the part that knew to order steak rare, and at a certain kind of restaurant a certain kind of wine, but at other occasions to be as downscale as possible, was responsible for the way he singled Anna out. Her exquisiteness. That he saw what I saw in her art. It was unimaginable to me that he didn't. Here we all were at Harvard, after all. Even though he was an Ec major, considered the most bullshit specialization possible at the school, it seemed to me that he ought to have had a broad enough background, a fine enough sensibility from all his prep school classes in history, literature, French to know what he was looking at.

Anna wasn't a conventional beauty. Despite her good figure and the restlessness that kept her in shape, her hair was ragged and flyaway, her color uneven. She could look worried, angry, certainly preoccupied. In our circle she would zone out of entire conversations. She slept erratically. Sometimes there were circles under her eyes. Often she was pale.

Suddenly she would dazzle. Show up in a shirt that was just the right fit or the right color or both. Get the right amount of sun or sleep. Crack everyone up with hilarious, perfectly timed, dry remarks, sarcastic impressions of political leaders or your closest friends whom you secretly resented. After a few days of this, she would disappear for days or weeks. She wasn't crazy in any kind of "look at me, I break all the rules" kind of way. She was no manic pixie girl; she wasn't enchanting. She certainly wasn't needy. I don't think she even noticed the irregularity of her behavior. She was on when she felt like it and off when she didn't. After all, she was making art that teachers associated with one of the finest museums in the world already were beginning to remark upon. If she acted like a human being in the margins, surely that was a bonus.

Those days when she showed up with her hair around her shoulders—later it would hang down her back—shot with a bit of copper from the sun, a touch of lipstick catching the natural flush on her cheeks, those days I would find every excuse I could to stand close, to play the straight man for her punch lines, to hand her another drink, though as a rule she did not drink as much as the rest of us did. She was too driven for that. She liked to leave open the possibility that she might work later in the night; she always feared that too much alcohol or pot would cause her to wake up the next day too disordered to be productive.

What did John see in her, if not what I saw? Perhaps he was just following us. Perhaps he felt he could not "get" a hippie chick on the order of Penny, his second wife. That popular, rich kind we had back then, the center of every group. Flat-chested and flat-bellied, with thick, wavy hair, wearing India-print skirts, ankle bracelets, frayed sleeves they drew down past their hands. He noticed that some of the time Anna was the star, and she was interested in him, so he went for it? Did I make it up, the love I had imagined flaring up between them? Would it have been possible, after all, for it to have been *me* who approached her at that party? But then again, would I have done so, without John's interest to draw my attention to her? My first impression of her had been that she was drab. My eyes had skated over her.

How quickly we became invested in the lives of our friends. Groups coalesced around couples.

A friend said to me recently: All my adult life I have been in love with my husband's best friend, since before we were married. She said: I saw him a few weeks before the wedding and I told myself, I will make this as obvious to him as I can. If it flatlines, I will go ahead and marry Benjy. Later she asked herself how she could ever really know if she had made herself perfectly clear to him. Already he thought of her as belonging to his best friend. Would he have allowed himself to absorb the signal even if she'd stripped naked in front of him? He'd probably have told himself she was getting ready to go skinny dipping.

What risk was I really prepared to take with Anna? I didn't push when she said no to me that night. I didn't tell her how I felt. Who knows how I felt anyway; I was a kid. She was John's girlfriend; I was his roommate. I wanted what he had.

7.

FELIX WAS THE LAW. He brought her into the hospital himself, in the back of his squad car, just as he had the first time. He was described as carrying her in tenderly, or at least solicitously. No one said she was struggling or trying to get away from him. She'd seemed dazed, and in fact she must have been in a scrim of pain from the re-fractured ankle, the repeated concussion, the rest of what had happened. Apparently he was counting on her not to report that. She didn't, at first.

But the village would know. I realized how much I myself knew. The Tanner girl he'd pushed face down in the mud in the middle of the Gillingham Fen. Already more than one babysitter. The continual harassment of the gay couple who owned that pale green cottage over on Todd Pond. Had I heard actual stories? I swear this knowledge was just in the air, hanging from the undersides of the leaves of the maples and elms.

The call came to the house at 11 PM because John was working late and not answering his office phone. I had just arrived. I'd already realized something was wrong. I had a good idea of what it was. *He'd have to kill me.* I'd stood in the broken door of the studio and looked up toward Baldy wondering how the hell, in these woods and swamps, you would ever find anyone, find a native son. Find him in time.

I tried John first, got no answer, tried dispatch, got a deputy. I asked for Felix, was told he had the night off. I said we'd had a break-in at Perkins

Ridge. The deputy said he'd be over in a jiffy. While he was examining the damage to the studio, the knocked-over canvasses and jars, I explained how Felix had been coming up and disturbing our peace. This deputy, a thin dark-haired boy who said he'd actually gone to a police academy, began by questioning me. What time had I left Dartmouth, had anybody seen me at my professor's office, could anyone verify my time of departure (the timestamp on my parking stub could). That's when the hospital called. I tried John one more time. "Follow me," said the deputy. I hopped into the Saab, chasing his shattering light the thirteen miles to Lansing.

When we arrived, Felix was sitting in his car, talking on his radio. The deputy went up to him with his hand over the gun at his waist.

"Hold it, hold her there," said Felix. "Don't do no fancy western shit. I'm yer boss."

"I don't care for that," said the deputy. "You're lucky no one came after you where the courts couldn't follow up on them."

Felix spat on the tar. "Right. John Perkins, rider of the apocalypse."

"You'll see," said the deputy, "Get out of that car."

"That man was not treating her one little bit right. He can't even treat a horse right."

"Okay, man. Get out of the car."

Felix unwound and let himself be handcuffed. The deputy clipped the handcuffs to the cage in the backseat, pushed Felix back inside, locked him in.

Only the deputy was allowed into Anna's room. As I understood it later, she wouldn't talk to him at first. I heard his voice raised with frustration and her in there crying. I pushed on the door. He came out then and agreed to stop until John could get there. It was now after midnight. I tried the house and he answered, groggy.

"I didn't wake you, did I?" I asked.

"Where's Anna?"

I explained as best I could.

"How did this happen?"

I found myself feeling defensive. "You'll just have to get over here," I said.

"Was she raped? Just tell me if she was."

I had a feeling rising through my body. In my gut or my groin. A dirty, bloody wave, a swelling I was choking on from the inside out, from the bottom up. "I don't know," I said. "I think maybe." I dropped the handset on its white cord and doubled over to retrieve it.

All those abduction stories: Guinevere carried off by Maelgwyn, Maid Marian caught by the sheriff, Mary raped by Rob Roy's nemesis. To recapture his woman, the lover must cross knife-like bridges, scale high walls, chop the bad guy in half. If he negotiates these obstacles well, the love is there waiting for him, behind the castle wall, deep in the dungeon. It's still there, the same true love he felt before she was stolen away. But there must have been stories, not passed down through the ages, when the task was just too great. There's some twist the hero didn't understand until too late, a code he couldn't break. Or the princess didn't wait long enough. What happens then, to that love?

People do write, or tell, or sing, the first kind of story, though, because of the miracle of having been in the presence of that kind of love. Flesh as the fingertip of the soul. Deflector shields down. The unguarded moment. What I believed in, from the first, about John and Anna's connection.

John went to his office nearly every day in the weeks of Anna's recuperation. Anna didn't repeat her effort to maintain her momentum in the studio. Her back-seat painting had been torn in the scuffle. Later, years later, she would return to it, on a fresh canvas, working from memory. The final result would win a major prize. I saw her—the only time I've seen her since New Hampshire—at a gallery show and expressed my amazement that she hadn't let the original vision be lost. "It's discipline, that's all," she'd said. "You keep a picture in your mind and wait for the mood to come around. If it doesn't, after a while you force it."

The concussion was worse the second time around, Anna's headaches and vomiting more frequent. John and I converted the dining room into a bedroom so she wouldn't have to negotiate the stairs. I rose before either of them did, hurrying up Baldy in the morning twilight to tend the seedlings that were already poking out of the soil. The plants needed twelve hours of daylight and this was the only time of year at this latitude when they'd get it. Before Labor Day I'd have to move them into the shed, where there'd have to be a complicated array of lights, heaters, and fans. I'd need to figure out irrigation up there too, a pipe from one of the small, year-round streams. So: up before dawn, race up the mountain carrying whatever supplies I could manage each time, weed, feed the plants, dig as much trench from the closest brook as I had time for, or build as much of the winter lighting structure as I had time for or had brought materials for, then race back down the mountain, see what Anna needed, because John was probably gone. Breakfast? Fresh water? A book by the bed in case her headache lifted? Help getting to the bathroom? Someone to hold her hair back while she puked?

Yes, I even did that a few times. John should have been there. I don't know why no one ever confronts John—it's as if we're intimidated by him, for some reason, and also are trying to protect him in some way. John had yelled at the deputy in the hospital. I'd never heard him raise his voice before. Now they were going through channels. Felix Chappell was in jail, awaiting trial. I didn't know what arrangements had been made because John talked to the lawyer from his Lansing office. I'd been told I might have to testify about the state of the studio when I'd come home that night. I might have to say something about Felix's earlier visits, about the non-protocol emergency trip to the hospital in the first place. I would be coached as the trial date approached. Every night John sat beside Anna and drilled her, so she wouldn't say anything stupid due to the strain.

"I don't want to testify," Anna told me after several days of vomiting.

"Most people don't in cases like this."

"It's not that. I don't care what people in this town think."

I handed her the toothbrush and a cup of water. She gagged a little but got her mouth clean. "They all know what Felix is like anyway. I don't think they'll mind if he goes to jail," she said.

"Maybe you should have a scan or something. Of your skull. You're throwing up too much," I said. I pulled the sheet up around her neck and got the pillow positioned under her ankle. "Did they ever check for a fracture?" I stroked her hair, which was slightly dirty. My fingers circled her temple.

Her eyes had been drifting shut. "It might not be the concussion," she said.

I kept my hand on her head, but my fingers stopped moving. "Are you sure?"

"No."

"Have you talked to John?"

"What would be the point. I've been having dreams, the kind women have. Knitting baby sweaters, infants crying in the background while I ransack the house for milk or apple juice because my breasts have mysteriously disappeared. Giving birth to dogs and cats. The thing is, it might be John's. Statistically, that's more likely. I hate those stories where a woman has sex with someone once, and wham."

"Can't they test whose it is somehow?" I said.

"Not until too late."

I pictured a child born with curly red hair. The whole town watching. I tried to imagine John affixing the Perkins name to it, as I would later see

Rob Roy doing in the movie.. "Maybe in this case the dreams are wrong," I offered. "Maybe they're just fears, not premonitions."

"Yeah," she said. She turned her head away and I understood that tears were flowing. A diversion of her life from mine. Possibly from John's as well.

8.

I LEFT HER AND DROVE TO DARTMOUTH. My mind had veered years ago at the thought of John and Anna having sex. Now I couldn't help thinking about it. John had mentioned plans for a family, but I'd supposed that was still in the future. She'd still had the first cast on, and they'd already been trying to have a child? Doggie style, I supposed. She always wore those loose Levi's jeans. I still wanted to know what her ass looked like under them. Did she wear that white cotton underwear, or had she grown a little more playful underneath? Had John?

What had Felix discovered when he pulled it off? Each morning when I helped her to her to bed in the dining room I'd thought about her thin nightgown under the sheet. Cast or no. I had a girlfriend one summer with a broken collarbone. Another, later, who broke her femur skiing. There are positions, there are angles. I doubted Felix had been so inventive. I found myself thinking about that too. That she had cried out, that she had fought, in pain, that he had not been troubled. It was if my binocular vision had stopped working. It did that, sometimes, when I was tired. Once, I'd gone to the eye doctor hungover. I'd always had 20/20 vision, but that day, when I looked through his machine at a green ball I saw two. He asked me how far apart they were and I said, "About four inches." He laughed and told me there was only one ball.

As I drove I might as well have been seeing two balls. The man holding one green ball was furious that someone could hurt a woman, hurt Anna so much. The broken bone, the concussion, the risk of pregnancy. The man holding the other green ball had a cock that was thickening. Just at the license of the thing. At the thought of being someone who was that free. Not to care, not to give one shit. Someone who might, all those years ago during that snowstorm in college, have stuck two fingers into Anna and seen what she had done *then*.

But I hadn't been that guy.

I can hear my father, the judge,say it: this Felix, he was out of context, that's all. This is not exactly the time and place for my father, speaking of out of context. He was a war hero, purple heart, medal of honor for pulling three men out from under the line of fire. You almost never get the medal of honor if you live. Went in, brought one out, went back, got another, went back again. He was wounded twice. Two of those three men survived. When I was sixteen and puffed up, running with the football boys, he pulled me aside, said, Don't get carried away by heroism. It's context. In the context of battle I did what a lot of people did.

His voice trailed off there. Later I thought he'd been about to tell me something really interesting. You don't think to ask the members of the Greatest Generation what they did in the war. Not the Americans, not the Brits. Not the good guys. In college, though, I read accounts of American soldiers gang-raping German women, strafing refugees. I asked my father about some of this after hearing an Austrian Buddhist describe being strafed while running home from school. By an American aircraft flying so low it had to be clear the targets were kids. "Yes, I can believe it," he said. "Context of war. They were our enemies, most guys didn't care if even the civilians survived. We wanted to go home." Without owning up to anything in particular, except to mention how willing the French women were, how open to the advances of Americans, he said, "No, I don't feel guilty. It was who we were then, it was *freeing*. But now here we are in regular life and that kind of behavior would be out of context, even a turn-off. If I had a gang rapist before me, and if the law would allow, I'd sentence him to death. I wouldn't feel like a hypocrite doing it."

My father was a lawyer and then a judge, a gentleman in every respect, a gentle man. A little strict with the money.

Were you a gang-rapist in a different context, Dad? I didn't ask.

One guy with one green ball wanting Felix in jail for life for what he did. All of me, in fact, wanting that. The second guy with the other green ball understanding, finally, what my father had said. This wasn't war. It wasn't in context. And maybe there were some men in the war who were disgusted, who didn't join in. *They* were out of context. Maybe it wasn't two percent of the population who were sociopaths. Maybe it was 2 percent in most of us.

Fifty percent says the second man with the second ball, but I know he's wrong. He's only standing there, free and clear because of some catalyst, just like I had to have that hangover to see the two green balls in the eye doctor's machine. For my father, the catalyst was war, for Felix it was probably being Felix, or the circumstances of his upbringing. And then the sheriff's star, the power vested in him. For me it was coming into proximity and anyway, I was just *seeing* the second green ball, having a few thoughts about it, feeling my dick thicken up just a little. Nothing anyone would see if I happened to stand up, nothing I was going to *do* anything about. I was having an experience, a moment of wonder, where you think, how is that even possible, that someone could be so free, *that they could just take what they want,* without even stopping to feel another person's pain.

My father had suggested it was possible not only to do this, but to exult in it, in a certain context, and in another, to punish a man severely for it. I hadn't understood him then. Here I was looking through two different eyes. Though different eyes of my own. I could *feel* myself hurting someone I loved. I wasn't just making a little movie of a cashier. I was *in* a movie about a friend. I was halfway hard over it.

When the deputy pulled out from behind the billboard on the perfectly straight section of 107 after you get off I-89, I was going 100 mph. It was broad daylight and there were no other cars on the road. The speed limit was 55, thank you Jimmy Carter. It's true the Saab was no Targa. And fair enough that I was well over the limit. Also so typical of New Hampshire cops, hiding away in spots where it does no harm to hit the accelerator, instead of in places where they might actually do some good.

I was so jacked up on my thoughts that I had to force myself to breathe far past my chest and count to ten while he was getting out of his car.

"Hello, it's you," the deputy said. "I thought I knew that funny-looking car."

"Sorry, man," I said. "Got lost in my thoughts, didn't think about my speed."

"Still need to see the license, registration. How's Mrs. Perkins?" he asked while I dug for the paperwork.

"She's still pretty battered," I said. "Concussion seems bad to me, but I'm sure John's on it. He doesn't want to talk about it."

"Husbands can get strange after things like this. That part might be hard for her, too."

I hoped he wasn't going to start looking in on her suddenly too.

"It's a mess," I said.

"Best to get the court date over with, get him put away."

"We can all agree on that," I said.

He wrote me a ticket, a big one, the bastard. But at least he didn't look in my trunk, where he would have found some of the pipes and other growing paraphernalia.

Later I had to explain it to John. I didn't have the money for a $45 ticket. John was calmly perplexed. Why would I be traveling with all that stuff in my trunk? Why had I not, after purchasing it, driven straight home—at exactly the speed limit—and unloaded it immediately? "John," I said. "I had stuff to do. I wasn't *thinking*."

John loved it when smart people didn't *think*. He paid the ticket.

"I'll pay you back," I said.

"Oh, don't worry about it. When you're rich, you can take me out to dinner."

9.

PENNY, TINA, AND I DRIFT BY CANDLELIGHT into the library. John hasn't emerged from his office. The library shelves are artfully arranged, not too book-heavy. Just the way they tell you to, if someone comes in to stage your house for sale. It makes the shadows in the room more strange. A certain number of "tchotchkes"—in this case, very fine items such as pewter mugs probably made by Paul Revere, vases, glass inkpots, quill pens—are interspersed with nicely bound hardcovers, arranged compatibly by color and size. Personally, I like a bookshelf to have a lot of books on it. Tina's and mine are packed. Our books are arranged by subject or author, depending. So I don't have to think: was *Sometimes A Great Notion* in a red jacket or a blue one? I suppose many people now keep the books they actually read on their Kindles. The rest are for show.

Sliding my candle along the shelves in this random manner, I come to green. *Ivanhoe*. And, of course, *Rob Roy*, by Sir Walter Scott. My hand shakes a little. "Can we start on that scotch?"

"Just because you've reached the Scottish shelf?"

"You might say that."

She hurries away.

Oh, Rob Roy again, I think, waiting for the whiskey. That goddamned hero. I try not to think of Liam Neeson swinging his broadsword over his shoulder. Off to slice a man right in half. Who has raped his wife. Tina weeping, during the movie, when he claims that child.

But Rob Roy is a legendary man. People make up stories about him.

"Thank you," I say, when the Cragganmore comes.

"Did you ever sleep with Anna?" Penny asks me, right in front of my wife.

"No," I say. It seems there is a concrete answer after all. "Anna and I did not sleep together."

"You probably wanted to, though," Tina says with a laugh.

"If so, that was ages ago, when I was a young and horny man."

Tina turns to Penny. "Don't you think all men want to sleep with their best friend's girls?"

Penny opens her mouth extra wide, in a kind of parody of a dropped jaw. I'd noticed this mannerism over the years. She uses it sometimes to play dumb, and sometimes to chide you, to let you know you'd dug too deeply.

"I think they do," Tina goes on. "At least, that's how it often seemed to me. I'd barely break up with some guy and presto, his friends would hit on me. Sometimes it could turn into a date rape situation. You'd have to be on your toes."

They both look at me again.

"No," I say. "And Anna certainly never betrayed anybody."

"Really," says Penny.

"Really."

"Yet, there's some wound John still carries, all these years," she says. "The paintings everywhere, and in the attic."

"In the attic?" Tina says.

"He's got three more paintings in the attic," the new wife says. "And he burned a few. He said it was best for her career if he did that. There was an article about the missing work in *Artforum* recently, speculating on where they were. He's seen as her nemesis, you know. The National Gallery wants to buy at least one of those attic pieces. He won't even say he has them."

He'd *burned* her work?

"He burned her paintings?" Tina says. Her face is red. "Doesn't that bother you? Isn't that a little nasty?"

"Nasty?" Penny says. "I have no way of knowing if it's nasty. I never met her. I don't know what happened."

I can't respond. Can't open my mouth.

Tina gestures to another Anna painting in the library, the gun factory with its shot-out windows. You can't really see it with a candle, but we get her point. "How does he burn her work? I don't care what happened. You don't burn *art*."

"He thought it was best for her career," Penny repeats. "He still tries to call her, whenever he sees an article, to offer his advice."

"That would drive me nuts," Tina says. She'd put down her drink a while ago.

"Your ex-husband calling you, or your husband calling an ex-wife?" I ask.

"It's the advice thing that gets to me," she mutters. Then, more loudly: "Both. But I wouldn't stand for you calling up your ex-wife."

Penny shrinks, finally picking up on our censure. She does that jaw drop thing again. "It's who he is," she says. "He's got to do this father thing with everyone. She's like the prodigal daughter."

"You don't think that's a little creepy?" Tina pushes. "That he sees his ex-wife as a kind of daughter?"

Penny turns aside. "He relates to everyone like that. Even you: he takes a caretaker role with Ethan, too."

"And I find it creepy. If you must know."

"Yet you still come around, like everyone else."

"Yep. I want to see how the old man is getting on."

"Come on," she says. "Let's just eat."

We follow her flickering light back down the hallway, past the pictures of the beautiful children. I sit in one of the straight-backed chairs. I'm glad we'd elected to bring salad and dessert, nothing that needed to stay warm.

"Do you like what you do for a living now?" Penny asks.

I look at Tina, relieved. Perhaps we will return to ordinary conversation subjects now. "Sure, I like my job." I actually do like it. Halfway through my second year of business school, I'd left Dartmouth for law school at Columbia. For the past twenty years I've been a litigator for investment firms. I love the challenge of it, the in-court press. I don't risk anything of my own.

"I always thought you seemed more gentle than that," Penny says.

"Than what?"

"Than a corporate shark."

"We always used to think John was the nicest guy ever," I say.

She tucks her chin. "We're going to get pretty drunk if we keep waiting," she says. "You loved her at least, didn't you? Anna."

Obviously this subject is not going to get dropped. "Is John still on that phone call?" I jab my thumb toward his office.

"Who cares? More important than us. So, you really didn't sleep with her, even after the divorce?"

"No," I say, still regretting that fact.

10.

BEFORE ANNA LEFT PERKINS RIDGE, she found me up on Baldy one afternoon. She'd needed to get out and walk, she said.

"Stiff hike," I said. Her leg was barely out of the cast. She looked terrible, like after one of her worst nights back in college. I guessed she didn't know any other way to manage the noise in her head. Physical activity, even if her leg wasn't ready, even if she was still bleeding from the abortion.

"I'm all right."

It turned out she had known about the pot operation all along, having seen right through John's reflexive lies about it. "I hope you make a ton of money," she said.

"You'll see if we do," I told her. "It's an experiment."

"No, I won't." She told me she was leaving. She would be back for the trial, of course. Otherwise, she couldn't bring herself. She said the abortion was the last straw.

"It wasn't your choice?" I asked.

That northeastern composure fractured for a second or two. I watched sadness heave across her face. Only for a moment. As much as I'd resented Yankee impenetrability when I'd first come East, now I found myself relieved when they got themselves under control. She squatted down, dipped her hands in the brook where I was sinking the last bit of pipe.

Her jeans, I imagined, slid down low on her hips. I couldn't see because her shirt was long. "For certain reasons," she said, "I might have done it even if I knew it was John's. Or, with a different husband, I might have kept it, even if it was Felix's."

She stood, shaking the cold drops from her fingers.

I guessed, given that she was leaving, that her first choice would have been for John not to have been John.

Over the next few days, I helped her pack her paintings, while she made calls with forced good cheer to old professors and art school friends, all while John was working. At last both a place to stay and a job surfaced. As I helped her organize, the sheep went on grazing their meadows and two of the horses, the black and the bay, grazed theirs. Only Jaybird paced. I realized I had never passed on Felix's advice.

"What will you do with the horses?" I said.

"They were here when I got here. Didn't they belong to his parents?"

"What about that one, though?" I pointed out to Jaybird, trotting his circles. "Shouldn't something be done?"

She shrugged. "He's out of his mind."

I saw that she really didn't grasp it. It wasn't that she had no compassion, but that she slid in and out of focus in alignment with art.

"I'll talk to John about it," I said.

It was an art school friend, her new roommate, who drove up to get her. John was working. I stood in the driveway to wave.

When I did discuss Jaybird with John, I had to be careful. Naturally, I couldn't let on that the idea had come from Felix. I simply said that on my uncle's Colorado ranch some of the more difficult horses did better with a goat or a pony, and I'd read something similar about racehorses as well. "Huh," said John. "I want to get rid of that horse anyway. He's nothing but trouble, tearing up those barn boards and such. One day he'll hurt someone and we'll get sued." He sat quietly for some time, sipping his Molson. I read the paper. Something clicked for him. "I think I'll call up Rusty Chappell, see if his wife wants it."

It was a canny solution. I'm sure John thought of it as a generous offer that helped everyone involved come out ahead. Win-win. Suzy Chappell had lost her mare, but she'd kept back a filly or two. The gift of a stallion might be helpful as the trial of Rusty's son progressed, or as John went to develop lands that bordered on Chappell holdings, where some of the original surveys were centuries old and pretty sketchy.

I saw Anna three times after she moved out of John's house. Twice during Felix's trial, and once at the art show in New York, where I was only one of many admirers. Sometimes friends just drift apart. Those early friendships from college, especially after a divorce. You don't mean to take sides, but you wind up defaulting one way or the other. I had crops to harvest, then I needed John's advice for the following years of speculation around Todd Pond, which I had rechristened as a "lake" for my brochures. John rolled his eyes and drew his brows together, but in the end I was right. Right enough for me. The eighties and nineties were good to central New Hampshire. John made many millions on the bigger lakes. I came to nearly two million on my little one. John loved coming over to supervise the local teams jacking up foundations. If they weren't doing it right, he'd send over some of his workers. He'd let me use his discounts on gravel for better beaches and swimming areas where once there had been slimy mud. My old boss Rusty Chappell himself delivered some of that sand with a wink and a burley wave. To John's mind, I was doing a stupid thing, but he was happy to help me out.

I wasn't sure what I would owe in return, or what poor Classics-major Stickney might owe John for his motorcycle rescue after all this time, but I imagined it must be something. I would get a phone call. Perhaps something as simple as investment advice, help getting out of a fund that had a penalty, a string pulled for a child at a college where I knew someone on the board. Though so far none of that had happened. The kids were bright enough to do it on their own, perhaps.

All his phone calls to Anna: what was he trying to extract? What was her debt?

We are halfway through Penny's salmon, the table ablaze with candles. The rain has stopped. It's impossible to see outside, but somehow I feel there is a movement across the windows, where the meadow materializes in daylight. I stand up, cup my eyes, press against the glass.

"What is it?" Penny says, scurrying to my side.

"Nothing, I'm sure. Just a feeling." There aren't any branches that might have shifted in the wind. I open the door to the outside, letting in a cold blast that causes Tina to draw her sweater off the back of her chair. I look out for only moment. Seeing nothing, I close the door again.

"Bear?" Tina says.

"Ninety-nine point nine percent chance of nothing," I say. "Not sure why I did that."

"Probably the ghost."

"There's only one?" Tina says.

"Very funny, till you're here on your own late at night. Luckily John doesn't travel much. But there are other things to watch out for. You have to trust your instinct sometimes. Up here. We did get broken into last week. We weren't home. They didn't even take anything."

"Right before the MayRoy?"

"Yes, it's concerning."

"I'd say so," Tina says.

"I'm going after John," I say. I take a candlestick and march down the hall. I knock, turn the knob without waiting for an answer. John is making notes in his DayTimer by a camping lantern. I don't really remember a lot of power outages from my time on the Ridge, but in general power grids seem more vulnerable everywhere. Climate change I'm told—creating more events, while population increases tax the systems.

"Just finishing up," he says, his sinuses echoing pleasantly.

"No problem," I respond, "but we started without you. Soon it will be time to leave."

"Sorry," he says. "Business is rough these days. I'm sure you understand." I nod. I am certainly glad I'm not a fund manager or in real estate any longer.

"Look at that!" I say. In the left recess of the large rolltop, which John is about to close, is a black-framed photo of the Porsche Targa. Only a shadow in this light, a shape. "She's not completely gone, then."

"No, not completely. Right where she belongs," John says, locking the desk.

"Sorry, Penny," John says, kissing his wife. He picks up the bottle of Scotch, pours himself a double. "It's those Chappells again. Rusty and whatnot. It never stops. You try to help people out sometimes. You know the woodlot up over Eagle's Nest? He's claiming his land goes three hundred yards beyond the new survey. Wants to clearcut it. I've had to get an injunction." He winces. I know John would hate resorting to the law and formalities.

My wife and I now have our own camp on the lake. We belong to the Big Shire Lake Protection Association, which opposes all parties who want to develop Eagle's Nest Point. Indian artifacts had been found there. However, it's part of the Perkins holdings. John wants to build a multimillion dollar estate for a particular client. I know, from my summer of working with Rusty, how much the Chappells have relied on their timber resources as part of their long-term survival plans. Chappells have been in this area as long as Perkinses have. The Chappells' roots went back to the wrong king, though. A French one; I've lost track.

"Are the Chappells still breeding horses?" I ask.

John shakes his big, balding head in that sad way he uses for people who just can't get it right. "I tried to help. Gave them that gray stallion for free, you know. He had great papers. No good for riding, but at stud he'd be fine. But they couldn't keep up the fenceline, which caused all kinds of problems. Rusty finally shot him."

"That was quite a to-do," Penny puts in. "I thought Suzy was going shoot *him*."

"In the end it turned out okay. They both started going to AA. Gave up the horse operation, started growing Christmas trees. Rusty still logs. He picked up the gravel works again."

I think of the proud arch to Jaybird's neck, the dapples across his gray flanks, the black fetlocks. Just a pony, a goat. Felix, of all people, had known what to do.

Penny brings in our dessert from the kitchen. A chocolate soufflé Tina is famous for. It melts in my mouth. I feel Tina's eyes on me from time to time, evaluating.

I look past the candlelight into the darkness of the hilltop. I did all right and I like the way we live. Our apartment on the Upper West Side, our camp on the lake, our two sons in fine colleges, my Audi. Right enough for me. It's enough but I can't deny I still want what John has. This place, these paintings on my walls, but more than that, his certainty of possession. Then I stop for a second, looking back at Tina, at the question in her eyes. Which wife would I choose? Not Penny, of course. She isn't even on my radar. In my fantasy life, if I lived up here on Perkins Ridge, because maybe that's who I really am after all, the villain. Guy of Gisbourne, trying to take possession of Robin Hood's Locksley, or whoever that guy was who was trying to take down Rob Roy—who, now, would I choose as the woman at my side? Anna, the true love, the ideal, or Tina, the woman I know, my real love?

And so we arrive at the later phases of our lives. When we find we must let go of the last of our fantasies because they have become so convoluted we cannot place ourselves within them any longer. I can't drive faster than 85. Tina would never live on Perkins Ridge with me. Anna would never return to it. I would find the house too hard to care for alone. Of course, my ownership of Perkins Ridge was always out of the question, but now it has fallen past the point of coveting.

A certain kind of grief: mourning the things you no longer want, mourning *that* you no longer want them.

So why hadn't I at least gone after Anna, wooed her in the wake of her divorce? Look at how she never speaks to John, and it's said, never speaks of him. I imagine her with a separate cell phone with the number he thinks she has, a phone she never looks at. She never comes back here, not even to visit the lake. Gave up those critical works the National Gallery wants to buy, plus whichever ones he burned. No one has ever since seen that unfinished piece of the sunken steamer amid its predatory boulders and the moss-water light.

Sometimes good friends decide not to get involved romantically because it might risk screwing up the friendship. That wasn't what happened to Anna and me, afterward, in New York. Our eyes had met at the show, and I'd known then I might have invited her out for drinks. I asked her about the cruise car painting. She told me how it had developed. No topic, that I knew of, had ever been off limits to us. I didn't ask her out, though, and she didn't seem disappointed.

In a way there was too much baggage. She was a damaged woman. A sullied woman, I guessed. Not because of what Felix had done, exactly. I wondered how often men responded in a similar way—my way—to rape, but couldn't—or wouldn't—articulate it, even to themselves. This woman I had loved wasn't dirty because she was raped. *I* felt dirty. I was jealous of the rapist. I still fantasized about the rape sometimes. I even wished I were him.

I wished I were him. Sometimes I thought: I would go to jail for him.

I still see her by the stream, the loose waistband sliding. I think of overpowering her, taking her there, her eyes glassing from the concussion, her ankle still sore. Bleeding from the abortion, I don't care. My father in those battles with the iron blaze of blood all around.

Perhaps I have done her greater violences, if only in my mind.

ACKNOWLEDGMENTS

This book was begun during a residency at Phillips Exeter Academy and pecked away at during the years since. Thanks to the Bennett Fellowship selection committee, especially Ralph Sneeden, Todd Hearon, and Matt Miller. Thanks also to the library staff, and to Erika Plouff Lazure, David Weber, and everyone else who reached out to make my time there richer and less lonely. I appreciate my writing group in Glenwood Springs for their input into sections of this manuscript, especially Kristin Carlson, Debbie Crawford, Pat Conway, Noel Armstrong, Mark Batmale, and George Lily. Thank you, Dan Falatko, Adam Bohannon and the rest at Neutral Zones Press. So grateful to Grace Gepfert Cooper for the cover painting. I couldn't have asked for better input from Roy Kesey, Robin Black, Ralph Sneeden, Mike Czyzniejewski, and Scott Lasser. Blurbs take time and are hard to write; yours were stellar. Tony Passariello gave a lot of support. Love to family: my son, Julian Putnam, my mother, Margo Steeves, and my sister, Kathleen Hurley.

Special thanks to the dogs and cats steadfast during these years. I couldn't have done it without you.